Juggler

by

Peter Dixon

Illustrated by David Thomas

To Oliver

First published in Great Britain by Barrington Stoke Ltd
10 Belford Terrace, Edinburgh EH4 3DQ
Copyright © 2000 Peter Dixon
Illustrations © David Thomas
The moral right of the author has been asserted in
accordance with the Copyright, Designs and
Patents Act 1988
ISBN 1-902260-51-1
Printed by Polestar AUP Aberdeen Ltd

MEET THE AUTHOR - PETER DIXON

What is your favourite animal?
A dodo
What is your favourite boy's name?
Oliver
What is your favourite girl's name?
Debbie
What is your favourite food?
Beef on the bone
What is your favourite music?
Loud
What is your favourite hobby?
Not getting up in the morning

MEET THE ILLUSTRATOR - DAVID THOMAS

What is your favourite animal?
Gwen, my tabby cat
What is your favourite boy's name?
Hugh, my son
What is your favourite girl's name?
Lois, my daughter
What is your favourite food?
Hot Cross buns
What is your favourite music?
The Dam Busters' March
What is your favourite hobby?
Watching TV asleep

Barrington Stoke was a famous and much-loved story-teller. He travelled from village to village carrying a lantern to light his way. He arrived as it grew dark and when the young boys and girls of the village saw the glow of his lantern, they hurried to the central meeting place. They were full of excitement and expectation, for his stories were always wonderful.

Then Barrington Stoke set down his lantern. In the flickering light the listeners were enthralled by his tales of adventure, horror and mystery. He knew exactly what they liked best and he loved telling a good story. And another. And then another. When the lantern burned low and dawn was nearly breaking, he slipped away. He was gone by morning, only to appear the next day in some other village to tell the next story.

Contents

1 Betts Wets   1

2 Mrs Timms' Curtains   7

3 Passing the Blame   15

4 Working with Debbie   27

5 The Big Secret   37

6 Saving the Day   47

   Aftermath   57

Chapter 1
Betts Wets

On his very first day at Bowes School, Mark Betts wet himself. He did it halfway through assembly, just as one of the big junior girls was singing a song all by herself.

I remember him doing it because he was sitting right next to me. I remember shouting out, "Mark Betts is peeing!"

Miss Smart jumped up from her teacher's chair and took him off to the cloakroom.

I know it wasn't really Mark's fault that he wet himself. He was only a little boy. But he never forgave me for calling out.

From then on he was always looking for ways of getting me into trouble with the teachers.

Mark grew fast and that was a problem too. He was miles bigger than anyone else in our year. He liked to use his size and strength to get his way at nearly everything.

Worse than that, I was the sort of boy who grew very slowly. Mark was the star of the football team and judo club. I was often mistaken for someone half my age and I never got chosen for any sports team.

It was our bad luck to have the Betts' living next door. They were really awful and moaned about everything we did. They said Mum's chickens were smelly. They said our television was too loud. They called our shed ugly and our garden a jungle.

They grumbled about my brother Derek most of all. They hated his oily bonfires. They hated the stray dogs he kept. They hated the old cars he fixed in the front garden.

The Betts' house next door was brand new and very posh. They had a small swimming pool, a neat patio and were always having barbecues.

I wished we had barbecues. I loved the smell of those onions and sizzling sausages. Mr Betts always did the cooking and wore a big blue and white striped apron with DAD written across the front. I asked Mum if we could have a barbecue but she said no. They were too much trouble. I asked Derek and he said barbecues were naff.

One day Derek caused terrible trouble by throwing a dead chicken over the wall into their swimming pool. Mr and Mrs Betts and Mark came round with the chicken in a bucket and there was a dreadful row. Mr Betts swore. My Mum got very angry with Derek after they had gone.

I think Derek disliked Mark even more than I did. One day he wrote 'Betts Wets' on the side of their garage wall with some paint he got out of a skip.

Derek was like that. He just didn't care, but he was my brother and he was a fireman. A fireman! That's what I was going to be ... a leading fireman in the fire service. Yeah!

Chapter 2
Mrs Timms' Curtains

It was June – scorching, hot weather and school concert time. The school hall had been tidied, PE stuff hidden away and the floor polished. But most importantly of all, the new stage curtains had arrived.

To most people new stage curtains didn't matter much, but for Mrs Timms, our school caretaker, they were the most important item in the school.

They were light cream, in fact almost
white. They had taken ages to make. A
team of parents had spent evening after
evening fixing millions of small plastic
hooks to a special tape stitched across the
top.

These hooks fixed onto the hanging cable which ran across the top of the stage. A small electric motor moved the curtains along the cable. I was in charge of working this motor's start and stop button. That's why I loved the school concert!

I loved the concert even more this year because Debbie Cross had been chosen to be my helper. Everyone thought Debbie was the best-looking girl in the school. It was even

said that she went out with boys from the big school.

Of course, Mark Betts was always chasing after her. More than once I'd heard her squeals and laughter drifting from the Betts' swimming pool on barbecue afternoons.

Usually, Debbie was acting in the concert, dancing or singing, but she had had a bit of an accident on a dry ski slope and still only walked with the aid of a stick. Debbie's accident was my good luck. No one minded having Debbie Cross to help them.

And then like rain at a picnic, everything began to go wrong. It was due, of course, to my 'friend' Mark Betts.

The concert was to be on the Saturday evening and Mrs Timms was getting hot and bothered. There was too much to do.

First of all, they'd run out of curtain hooks. Then the curtains were too long, then they were too short and then the new hooks were the wrong shape for the holes they had to fit.

But by Thursday lunchtime all the problems had been sorted out and they were ready to be hung up.

They looked terrific, especially when Mrs Betts, in her role as Chairperson of the Governors, shone the violet-coloured stage light full on them.

Everyone clapped to thank the ladies who had fixed them and Mrs Timms was extremely proud of everyone's hard work.

It was then that the first disaster struck. It came from the man who had come to fix the speaker systems.

"That motor's shot. It's done for," he explained, pointing at the pulleys, cable and old electric motor. "If you switch it on it will chew all those hooks into little pieces ..."

One of the ladies who had spent four evenings helping to sew on the hooks turned as pale as the curtains and scurried off to tell Mrs Betts.

I felt rotten. I loved pressing buttons and doing things to do with technology and stuff like that. That's why I was going into the fire service, like Derek.

I tried to sort things out a bit. "If I just sort of press it ever so gently will it be all right?" I asked.

"No, it won't," snapped the man fixing the speaker systems. "The system is useless – it's too old. The only way you'll get those curtains opening and shutting is by pullin' 'em and pushin' 'em by hand." He picked up his bag importantly and strode off towards his van.

"Well, that's how it will have to be," explained Mrs Betts. "They will have to be pulled by hand but we ought to have someone very sensible doing it." She eyed me nastily and added, "I'll have a word with the headteacher about that."

And that's how Mark got my job. That's how Mark became head curtain boy.

Chapter 3
Passing the Blame

Mark knew he was one up on me, as he swanked onto the stage. His guitar swung at his side like a real pop star's. I envied him as much as I disliked him.

He winked at Debbie. "It's you and me then," he grinned, putting his arm across her shoulder. "When I'm not playing the rock numbers I'll be with you ..."

He eyed me and added, "Old titch can be a reserve. Just in case I have to change a guitar string or do an encore."

I didn't think Debbie looked all that pleased, but Mark didn't notice. He strolled over to the electric motor.

"Don't touch that!" I blurted. "It's not ..."

Mark spun round in anger. "Don't you tell me what to do you stupid squirt!" he shouted. "I'm in charge here and if I want to press buttons then I press buttons. I don't need your permission."

"But the man said ..." I continued. But I got no further.

Mark leapt towards me with fists clenched and would have knocked me flat on my back, if it hadn't been for the guitar.

A large guitar is an awkward object and Mark's legs were long and dangly. He staggered. For a moment I thought he would stay on his feet, but he tripped on the bits of wood left by the scenery builders and down he fell.

It wasn't the worst of falls, but to do it in front of Debbie was dire. Then there was the guitar. The crack of the instrument snapping was far louder than the thump of Mark's body. He jumped up in horror.

"My guitar! My Fender!" he bellowed. "He's bloomin' bust it!" There was spit and froth all over his lips and his eyes filled with massive tears. He wrenched the guitar strap over his head. Its neck hung down. A broken limb, strings swaying like limp boot laces. The scene was horrific.

It was Debbie who spoke first. "It's not his fault. He was only telling you that the man

said you weren't to press the curtain button.
The man said ..."

But that was more than enough for Mark.
"People like him don't tell me what to do!"
And with a stride he was beside the motor. He
paused for a moment, took a breath and
jabbed his thumb on CLOSE.

For a second nothing happened then there
was a buzz as the cogs and pulley wheels
heaved the cables into action.

Slowly and painfully, the curtains jerked across the stage. There were shocking sounds of splintering and splitting. Thousands of fragments of shattered plastic hooks rained down and bounced crazily across the stage and over the polished hall floor.

We stared in misery as the curtains gradually lost their grip upon the track and flopped down in huge, ugly folds. More and more hooks splintered and soon almost the entire curtain lay in a crumpled heap upon the stage.

There was a brief pause in the curtains' struggle and a dreadful grinding sound from above. A few more broken hooks fell to the ground and the motor gave a final, snarling tug at the pulley.

There was a blue flash, a stink of burning and then everything fell silent.

It was Debbie, once again, who spoke first. "See, we told you. We said not to push it."

Mark, for once, looked totally defeated, almost panicky with dismay. But he quickly composed himself. "*He* done it!" he shouted, prodding his finger in my direction. "He said to press it."

But by now teachers were on their way, with Mrs Timms at their head.

"I cannot believe it!" she shouted. "Someone tell me this isn't real!"

But it was real. The pulley system was wrecked. The curtains couldn't even be opened and closed by hand. There were no more hooks left and anyway everyone knew that there was no time to fix them before the concert.

One helper lady who had stitched and fixed for three long evenings was in tears.

Mrs Betts looked round for someone to blame. "It's *him*," she hissed, pointing at me. "It's *him*. First he smashed Mark's guitar and now he's wrecked the curtains."

****

It was nearly lunch hour and we were all sitting in the headteacher's study. Mr and Mrs Betts, two of the helper ladies, Mark and me. Mrs Timms was there too and she looked amazingly angry. Debbie had been sent back to class.

When she first arrived, Mrs Betts had shouted at me. She used words like 'vandal', 'hooligan' and 'troublemaker'. She even started to tell the story about the dead chicken being thrown in the swimming pool. She added that Derek had burnt old, oily

motorbike rags on purpose when they were having party drinks on their patio.

But Mrs Mills, our headteacher, was very stern with her. Mrs Mills said that it wasn't the right time for that sort of talk.

When Mrs Mills had heard both sides of the story, she decided that Mark had probably misunderstood what I said about the button.

The real problem was what to do about the school concert. There was a long pause.

Then Mr Betts spoke. He had a loud voice and his words came slowly and very thoughtfully, and this is what he said. "Tomorrow night will soon be here. We have no curtains. That means we can't hide the stage when we need to change the scenery in the halfway break."

Everyone looked thoughtful. Everyone was quiet. The clock ticked. Mrs Mills' goldfish swam slowly round its bowl.

Mr Betts went on, "Tomorrow night I suggest we ask everyone to leave the hall in the halfway break, so that the scenery can be changed."

"But where will everyone go?" asked Mrs Mills.

Mr Betts gave a little, clever smile. "They will all go into the playground. I shall arrange a barbecue. Nothing special, something simple. Probably just sausages and onions. Even a few chips ..."

"And ketchup," added Mark, licking his lips.

Everyone looked pleased.

"You can leave that all to me. Young Mark can help and so can some of his friends."

"We can bring the new chip fryer you bought in America," grinned Mark. "It does sausages in crispy batter too. They're lovely! Really yummy."

Mrs Mills beamed. The concert would go ahead. The Betts had saved the day.

Chapter 4
Working with Debbie

Now that we didn't need curtains and there was nothing much for me to do, I thought I'd be sent back to my class.

The stage, however, needed tidying and the pale cream curtains had to be folded and put away.

Mark, Debbie and I were chosen for the job. Mark was still going on about how I'd not explained things to him properly. Then he said ten times over that my Mum would have to pay for a new guitar. But he did boast that he had got two reserve ones at home. Then he seemed to forget about it.

Folding up the curtains was good fun because Debbie liked a laugh. We spent ages crawling right under them and standing up so that we looked like big, lumpy snowmen or sort of ghosts. Even Mark seemed quite jolly and time whizzed by until afternoon break.

Then something quite good happened. Mark was caught spitting by one of the playground ladies. Of course, Mark said he hadn't, but she marched him up to Mrs Mills' office and made him stand outside her door.

I don't think he had been spitting this time. But the playground lady never seemed to like Mark and everyone always felt pleased when he got in a row. Even when it was for something he hadn't done.

Debbie and I were left to do the curtains together.

We decided to sort out the rubbish left by the scenery builders first and do the curtains last of all. There wasn't too much to clear up. Apart from the broken hooks, it was mainly scraps of wood and tins of paint.

"Your brother's a fireman, isn't he?" Debbie asked. "He came to my auntie's house when her cat got stuck up the chimney. I really liked him. I was at Mr Betts' house on that Sunday when Derek kept looking over the fence with that funny monkey mask on. Mrs Betts got ever so angry. The more she told him to go away the more he went on doing it. I think your brother's a real laugh ..."

She paused and looked a bit dreamy. "He got right up on that branch of your tree that hangs over their garden and pretended to be a chimpanzee scratching his bum! Yes, he's a real laugh your brother ..."

I knew all about the dead chicken and the oily rags and I knew that Derek had quite a few daft masks, but I never knew about the monkey mask. Mum would have killed him if she'd known!

I felt it was my turn to say something interesting about things I did, but I couldn't think of anything much. So, I said, "Derek can juggle."

Debbie looked at me as if she was expecting a bit more, so I added, "He can juggle with anything."

"Can he juggle with flaming torches?" she asked.

"Yeah – and broken bottles, bananas, old boots or, or, or … well, just anything," I added.

"What about dead chickens?" Debbie laughed. "Can he do it with them?"

"Anything," I grinned. "He can juggle with anything."

"Mrs Betts' best knickers?" she squealed. "And how about old Betts' barbecue sausages?" Debbie's face was going pink with laughter and her yellow hair swayed across her face.

"I can juggle too," I announced.

"Can you really?" She looked surprised.

"Yeah – I can juggle anything, anything," I continued.

"Anything?" she asked.

"Anything," I repeated.

"As good as Derek?" she persisted.

"Better than Derek," I boasted.

She gazed at me thoughtfully. "You don't look much like Derek, do you?"

"Well, no, but Derek's Dad was black. He came from Barbados. My Dad's Irish."

There was another little pause. Then once again her laughter trilled. "Let's see you juggle then ..."

And that's how I found myself centre stage with three tins of paint in my hands.

****

The truth was that I'd never juggled anything in my life! Debbie came really close. I could feel her breath on my cheek.

"Let me see you throw the tins really high," she whispered in my ear. "Just like you said Derek does. Like Derek ... right up, right up high. So I can watch them spin and twist."

Up, up, up they went. One seemed to touch the ceiling. As I threw them up, Debbie's whoops sang in my ears ...

I think I really did believe I'd catch them as they fell down. It was that sort of feeling you get when a footballer hits the back of the net or tennis players serve aces. It always looks easy-peasy. You always think you can do it too.

Well, up the tins went and as they rose, panic hit me. My eyes misted over, my palms went wet and slippery and somehow or other

my feet refused to move. I almost caught the first tin, but it hit my arm and rolled under the stack of chairs. Debbie snatched at the second, but the third tin fell free.

When it hit the stage floor there wasn't much of a noise. It didn't crash or thud, or even make a metallic clank. In fact, I didn't actually hear anything at all.

It's what I saw that I remember. It's what Debbie saw that she talks about. The paint shot out of the tin like a long, red, glistening snake or a flame. First it twisted and whirled up towards the ceiling and beyond. Then it stopped its climb and seemed to pause. It even seemed to be looking around.

Then, with one awful plunge, it hurled itself upon the pale cream curtains. A red and ugly kiss of death.

Chapter 5
The Big Secret

Curtains soaked in thick paint are not easy to clean. In fact, they are impossible to clean.

Debbie and I tried scraping spoonfuls of red paint from the curtains. After five minutes, we both gave up. It was hopeless. The curtains were ruined and we both knew it.

Almost without speaking we folded them into a bundle with the ruined part hidden in the middle. We placed them in the corner near the playground door and sat down.

The great pile of expensive cream curtaining looked fine. It looked perfect. It looked just as a brand new set of folded curtains should look. But deep in the middle, still gently soaking through, was the heart of a dreadful secret Debbie and I shared.

It was a secret we decided to keep until the concert was over. A secret too dreadful to tell Mrs Timms or any of the teachers that afternoon.

****

Next evening we sat together near the curtains as the hall filled with parents, governors and their families.

Mark had come in a fancy black suit and a little bow tie. Mr Betts was already getting his pans fizzling and flaming in the striped tent he had fixed up at the side of his camper van.

We didn't like to move away from the curtains in case anyone spotted the small, red stains that were already seeping out at some of the edges. But no one took any notice. We were left to sit and worry.

Debbie had brought her hamster along to cheer us up. This was nice, because the concert was really a bit boring. We couldn't see very well from where we were sitting.

He was called Hammy and until he escaped from my hand and disappeared behind the stage blocks, he was rather fun.

I was worried when he ran away but Debbie said he always turned up again.

Once Hammy had gone, I gazed out of the window. Mr Betts was very, very busy. Sweat was streaming down his face and he had huge tomato ketchup stains on his DAD apron. He had tied a little, white rag round his throat like a TV chef.

I could see huge piles of golden chips and wished that the school choir would sing a bit faster and that the interval would soon arrive.

I looked at the concert programme. There was one more act before the break and Mr Betts' sausages. It was called 'Rock with Mark'.

I could see Mark backstage sliding into his slippery, silvery Elvis suit, with 'Mark' in silver studs across the back. He saw us, gave a thumbs-up sign and showed us Hammy in his hand.

We watched him play around with the little animal, placing it on his shoulder and that kind of thing ... even putting Hammy on his guitar and pretending to play a tune.

But Mark was suddenly caught out. The choir didn't sing their last number. The show was running late and it was time for the school's answer to Elvis Presley.

The announcer took a large breath, put on a big smile and bellowed, "Ladies and Gentlemen, a big hand for Mark Betts!"

But Mark was late! He shuffled onto the stage still tugging on his jacket and holding his guitar rather awkwardly. There was a big cheer, then Mark was into his first number.

I didn't want him to be a good guitar player. I didn't want him to be a good singer, but he was. The audience loved him.

The louder they clapped the more he wiggled his hips and jerked himself around.

Then something began to happen, and it happened in his very quiet love song, the one about not being able to stop falling in love with you ...

I couldn't believe my ears because some of the teachers were beginning to laugh. First of all it was little sniggers, then quiet chuckles, then parents began to chuckle too and some laughed even louder.

Mark struggled on. He had closed his eyes. "... but I ca-a-an't help f-a-a-l-lin' in love ..."

By now almost the whole audience was in fits of laughter. And then Debbie and I saw why!

It was Hammy, good old Hammy, slowly climbing from silver sequin to silver sequin up Mark's trouser leg.

Mark battled on, eyes still half shut, head tilted to the stars as Hammy wriggled onto his belt and on to the collar of his jacket ...

By now Mark was losing his place. He had almost stopped playing. The whole audience was hooting with laughter and Mrs Betts had run on stage to grab the hamster and lead poor Mark off.

"Well, well, well!" grinned Mrs Mills. "I don't know if that was intended or not, but Mark certainly gave us a good last number. So it's interval time now. Enjoy your chips, sausages and ketchup thanks to our good friend, Mr Betts."

Chapter 6
Saving the Day

Mr Betts' chips were lovely, but the queue for sausages was very long. I had left Debbie guarding the curtains. We didn't want nosy parkers poking around at them and discovering what had happened.

But when I returned with her share of chips and ketchup she had bad news. The curtains were beginning to leak!

In all sorts of places, dark, reddish blobs were beginning to stain right through, and in two folded corners there were small, red trickles actually dripping onto the floor.

Of course, Debbie wiped them up, but we were only too pleased when the second half of the concert began.

Mrs Betts performed a soppy love song. After her, the school woodwind group played their recorders. Then it was the school choir again. After that, a father read a long poem. Finally, a group of infant kids did some dancing.

I was bored. I gazed at the background scenery of hilly countryside with a red sun setting behind the hills. I realised that the setting sun was done in the same red paint as I'd spilt. What a shame it hadn't all been used up. Then I'd never have done my juggling and we wouldn't have been in this mess.

The infant kids danced off and got told off for talking. The violins played a second time. They had gone wrong in the first half and now they were going to try to get it right. This time a teacher played in the back row. But it wasn't much better. Lots of people shuffled their feet and talked. I began to gaze out of the window into the playground.

Mr Betts had come into the concert hall and seemed to be enjoying the show. His camper van and tent stood silent, the cookers quiet.

Then something caught my attention. First of all, I thought it was the sun playing tricks, and then I thought it was red and silvery flapping paper. Then I thought it was something reflecting in the window panes. And then, suddenly, I realised it was none of those things. It was a fire!

One of the chip pans was slowly burning. Before I could do anything other than stare, it suddenly blazed into a massive fireball and the other pans caught light, threatening the tent and the camper van.

"Fire!" I yelled. "Fire! Fire! Fire!"

A moment of awful silence struck the hall. A hundred heads turned towards the playground, the flames and bellowing smoke.

"Water!" yelled someone. "Fetch water!"

A man grabbed a fire bucket and flung open the playground door. I threw myself against him.

"No!" I screamed. "Not on fat! Never throw water on a chip pan!"

The man stopped. I struggled to drag one of the curtains out into the playground. "Help

me!" I shouted. Others saw my idea and together we dragged the curtains out and hurled them over the three or four blazing pans.

The curtains were new and strong. Within moments the flames died down beneath their heavy folds. Soon firemen arrived and I was proud to see Derek amongst them.

"Luckily, you knew what to do," grinned the man in the white helmet. "But your curtains have had it."

"Don't worry about those," said Mrs Mills. "Our insurance will pay for them. They saved the day."

"And my camper van," laughed Mr Betts. "The boy is quite right, water would have made things far worse."

Everyone looked at me.

"I'm going to go into the fire service," I explained.

"Good thing too," smiled Mrs Timms. "Lucky you knew what to do. But my curtains have had it, that's for sure." She pulled a blackened length. Then she pulled at another not so blackened length. She stared at it in an odd sort of way. "That's funny," she added. "Lots of it seems all sort of covered in red stuff."

Everyone looked. Mrs Mills examined another piece. "I wonder what it is?" she said in a curious voice.

I fell silent, then like the voice of an angel, I heard Debbie.

"It's ketchup, Mrs Mills. I heard ketchup bottles exploding everywhere."

"Of course!" laughed Mrs Timms. "Ketchup. How silly of us not to realise that."

I could have kissed her. Not Mrs Timms – I mean Debbie.

The Aftermath

Mum

She got married
again to a chap called
Dave and we live in Swanage now. Dave and
Mum run a 'B and B' near the Red Lion pub
and I help.

Mrs Timms

She continued as school caretaker for three more years, but the curtains were never replaced. The insurance money (£800) was put towards a new computer.

The Curtains

All the bits with 'ketchup' on were chucked out. The other parts were used as dusters and rags.

Mr Betts

He bought the bottom part of our old garden and built a massive garage for his camper van. He cut down our trees to let more light into his garden.

Mrs Betts

Mrs Betts does not like the people who moved into our old house. They have got five cats that make messes on her lawn and sometimes on the patio.

Mrs Mills

She is still at Bowes School. She had the stage converted into an area for science and technology studies, but there are still small, red stains on the floor if you look carefully enough.

Derek

New people rented
our old house after we
left. Derek had to move. On the day he left
he let out all the chickens and chased them
into the Betts' garden. He still keeps in
touch with us.

Mark's guitar (Fender)

My Mum never paid for it to be repaired
and in the end Mrs Betts stopped asking.

Debbie

Debbie's leg got
better and she
moved away as well.
I don't know where she went. She said she
would write to me, but never did.

Debbie's hamster (Hammy)

I don't know what happened to it, but I think it might have died. It might have got away though.

Mark

Mark became school captain. Then he left to go to a private school in Yorkshire. He is going to be an insurance man.

Me

I still want to be in the fire service, but if I can't do that I'd like to be in charge of curtains and things in a theatre.

Derek's cars

They are still in the front garden of our old house. Mrs Betts still sends the council man round to look at them, because they attract rats.

The fire

It was on the front page of our local newspaper. It said, 'Boy's Fast Action Saves Disaster'. That boy was me.

Barrington Stoke would like to thank all its readers for commenting on the manuscript before publication and in particular:

Nigel Brown
Davina Howell
Kirsty Macleod
Andrew Morpeth
Sanjay Patel
Esther, Tim, Josh, Emily and James Ryley
Catherine Waite
Peter Wilkes

Barrington Stoke Club

Would you like to become a member of our club? Children who write to us with their views become members of our club and special advisors to the company. They also have the chance to act as editors on future manuscripts. Contact us at the address or website below – we'd love to hear from you!

Barrington Stoke, 10 Belford Terrace, Edinburgh EH4 3DQ
Tel: 0131 315 4933 Fax: 0131 315 4934
E-mail: barringtonstoke@cs.com
Website: www.barringtonstoke.co.uk

If you loved this story, why don't you read ...

The Two Jacks

by Tony Bradman

Are you always getting told off at school? Or are you the teacher's pet? Jack Baker is the perfect pupil until a new teacher mistakes him for bad boy Jack Barker. She even thinks naughty Jack Baker is the teacher's pet!

Will life ever be the same for the two Jacks?